Tiny Blue Baxter

by Bailey Carroll • illustrated by Carolina Farias

SCHOLASTIC INC.

Designed by Miguel E. Carvajal.

No part of this publication may be reproduced in whole or in part, or stored in a retrieval system, or transmitted in any form or by any means, electronic, mechanical, photocopying, recording, or otherwise, without written permission of the publisher. For information regarding permission, write to Scholastic Inc., 557 Broadway, New York, NY 10012.

Copyright © 2018 by Scholastic Inc.
All rights reserved. Published by Scholastic Inc.
Printed in the U.S.A.
Produced by Clean Slate Press Ltd.

ISBN-13: 978-1-338-26321-3
ISBN-10: 1-338-26321-8

SCHOLASTIC and associated logos are trademarks
and/or registered trademarks of Scholastic Inc.

D1377009

3 4 5 6 7 8 9 10   40   26 25 24 23 22 21 20 19 18

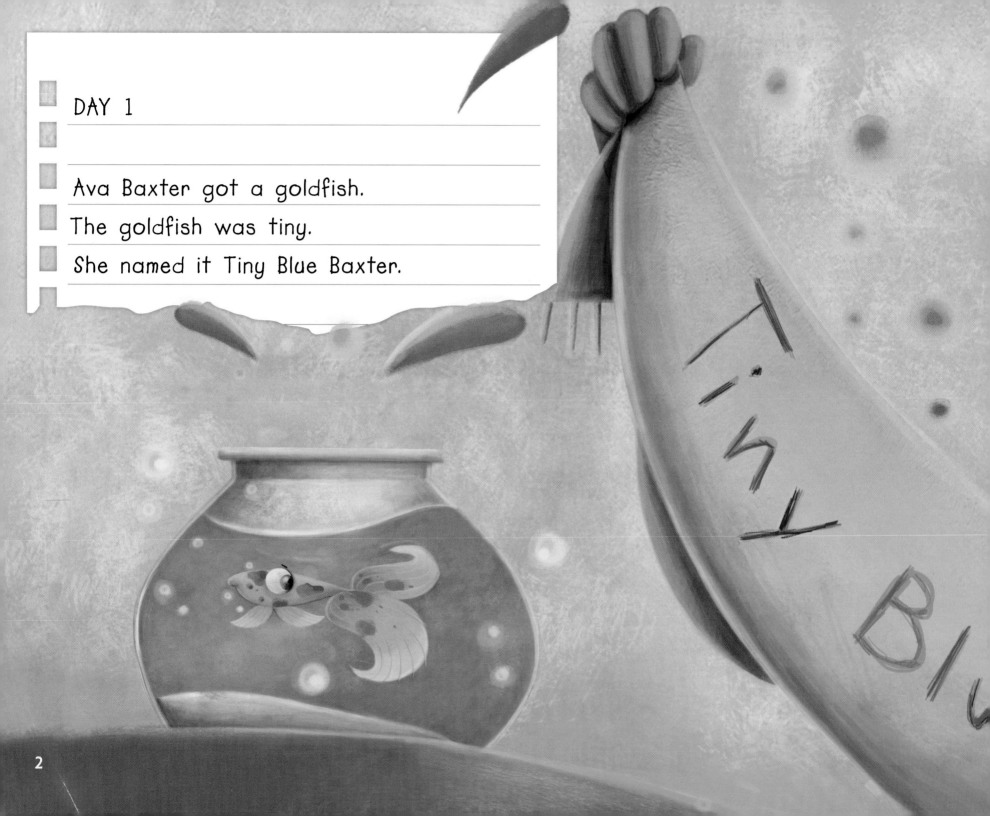

DAY 1

Ava Baxter got a goldfish.

The goldfish was tiny.

She named it Tiny Blue Baxter.

2

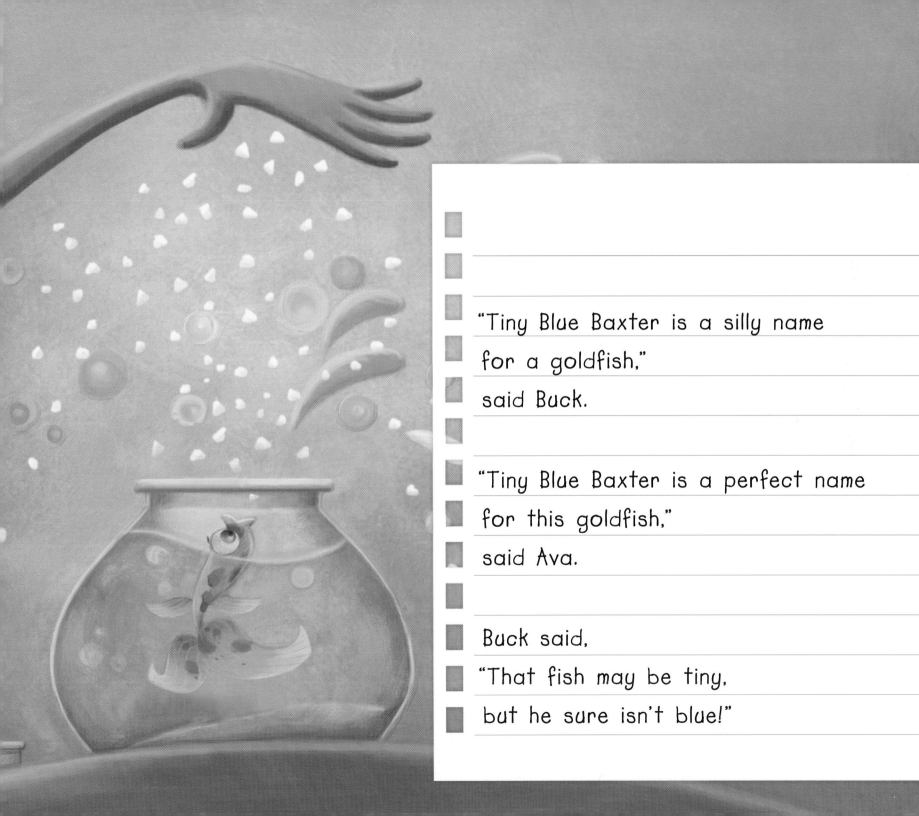

"Tiny Blue Baxter is a silly name
for a goldfish,"
said Buck.

"Tiny Blue Baxter is a perfect name
for this goldfish,"
said Ava.

Buck said,
"That fish may be tiny,
but he sure isn't blue!"

DAY 7

Ava fed Tiny Blue Baxter.
She fed Tiny Blue Baxter twice a day.

"Tiny Blue Baxter got bigger!"
said Ava.

Buck said,
"He sure did!"

Mom said,
"Oh, my!"

DAY 14

Ava said,

"I think Tiny Blue Baxter needs

a bigger bowl."

Buck said,

"I think Tiny Blue Baxter needs

a much bigger bowl."

"Oh, my!"

said Mom.

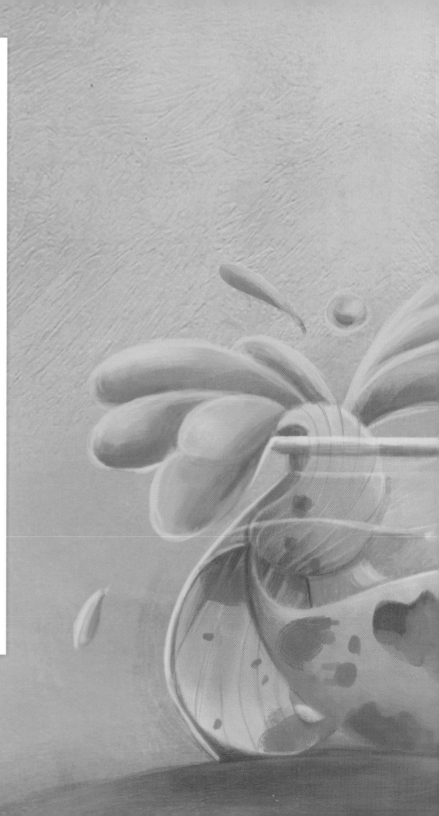

Tiny Blue Baxter liked the new bowl.

The new bowl was much bigger.

DAY 21

Ava Baxter fed her fish twice a day.
Tiny Blue Baxter got bigger and bigger.

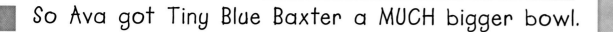

So Ava got Tiny Blue Baxter a MUCH bigger bowl.

Soon Tiny Blue Baxter got bigger and bigger . . .

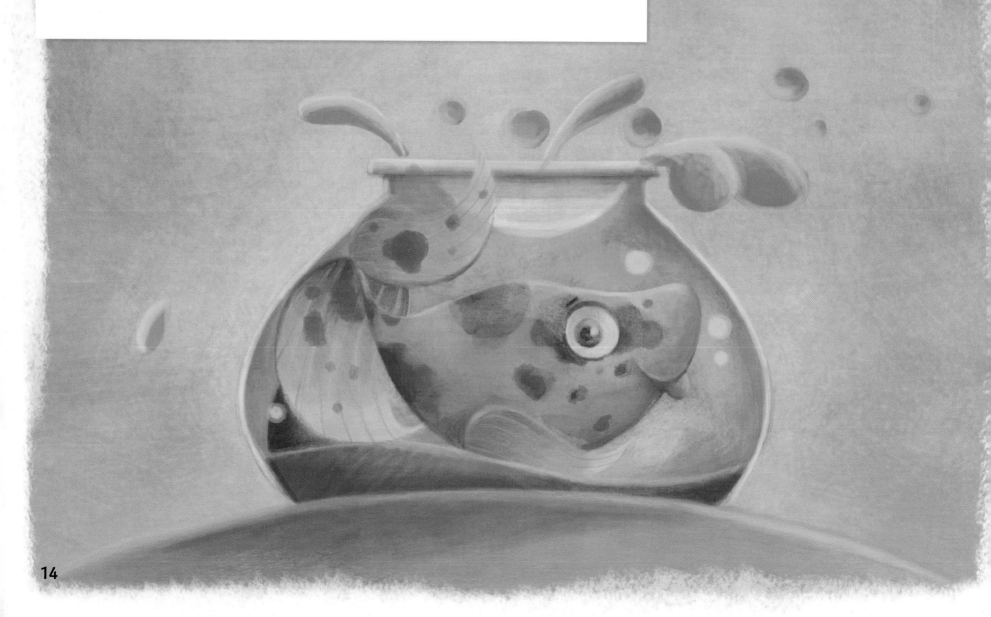

and bigger!

"Oh, my!" said Mom.

Tiny Blue Baxter was not blue.
And Tiny Blue Baxter was not tiny.
But Tiny Blue Baxter was the best goldfish
that Ava ever had.